THE STORM WHALE

The wonder of the world
The beauty and the power,
The shapes of things,
Their colours, lights and shades,
These I saw.
Look ye also while life lasts.

SIMON AND SCHUSTER
First published in Great Britain in 2013 by
Simon and Schuster UK Ltd, 1st Floor, 222 Gray's Inn Road,
London WC1X 8HB • A CBS Company • Text and illustrations
copyright © 2013 Benji Davies • The right of Benji Davies to
be identified as the author and illustrator of this work has
been asserted by him in accordance with the Copyright,
Designs and Patents Act, 1988 • All rights reserved, including
the right of reproduction in whole or in part in any form
A CIP catalogue record for this book is available from
the British Library upon request
ISBN: 978-1-4711-1567-7 (HB) • ISBN: 978-1-4711-1568-4 (PB)
ISBN: 978-1-4711-1569-1 (eBook)

THE STORM WHALE

Benji Davies

SIMON AND SCHUSTER
London   New York   Sydney   Toronto   New Delhi

Noi lived with his dad and six cats by the sea.

Every day, Noi's dad left early for a
long day's work on his fishing boat.

He wouldn't be home again till dark.

One night, a great storm had raged around their house.

In the morning, Noi went down to the beach
to see what had been left behind.

As he walked along the shore,
he spotted something in the distance.

As he got closer, Noi could not believe his eyes.

It was a little whale washed up on the sand.

Noi wondered what he should do.

He knew that it wasn't good for
a whale to be out of the water.

"I must be quick!" he thought.

Noi did everything he could to make the whale feel at home.

He told stories about life on the island.
The whale was an excellent listener.

The night was drawing in
and it was growing dark.

Noi was worried that his dad would be angry about having a whale in the bath.

Somehow, Noi kept his secret safe all evening.

He even managed to sneak some supper for his whale.

But he knew it couldn't last.

Noi's dad wasn't angry.
He had been so busy, he hadn't noticed
that Noi was lonely.

But he said they must take the whale
back to the sea, where it belonged.

Noi knew it was the right thing to do,
but it was hard to say goodbye.

He was glad his dad was there with him.

Noi often thought about the storm whale.

He hoped that one day, soon . . .

...he would see his friend again.